This
Little Princess Story
belongs to:

. . . .

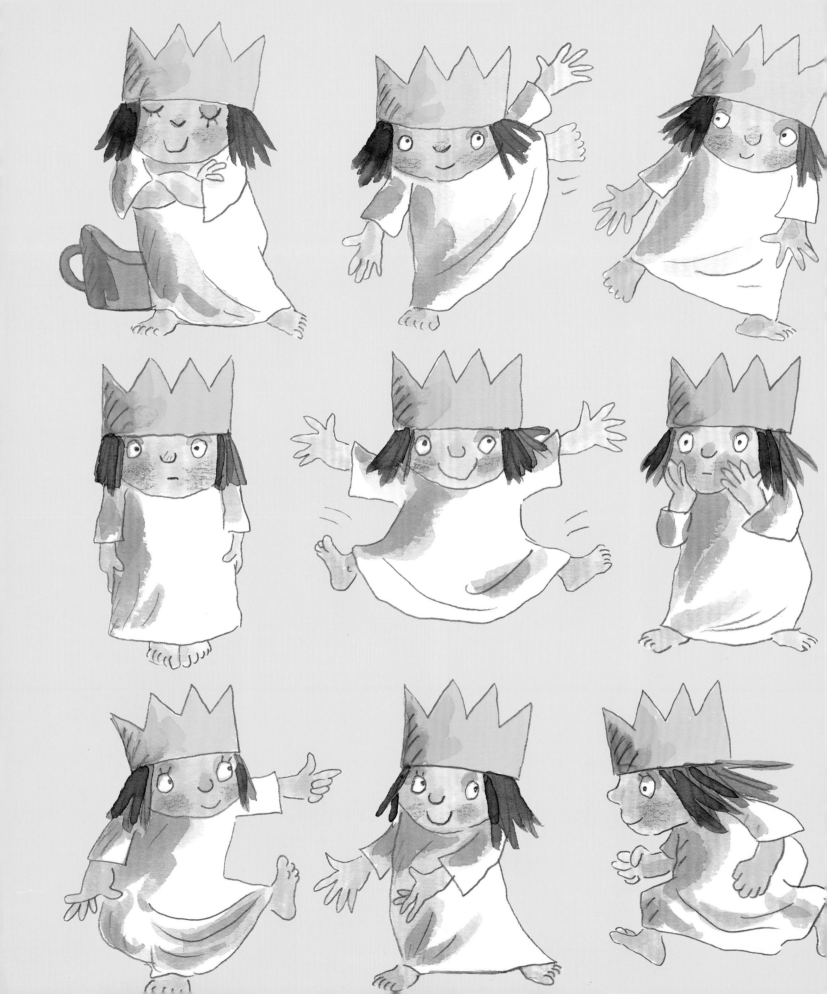

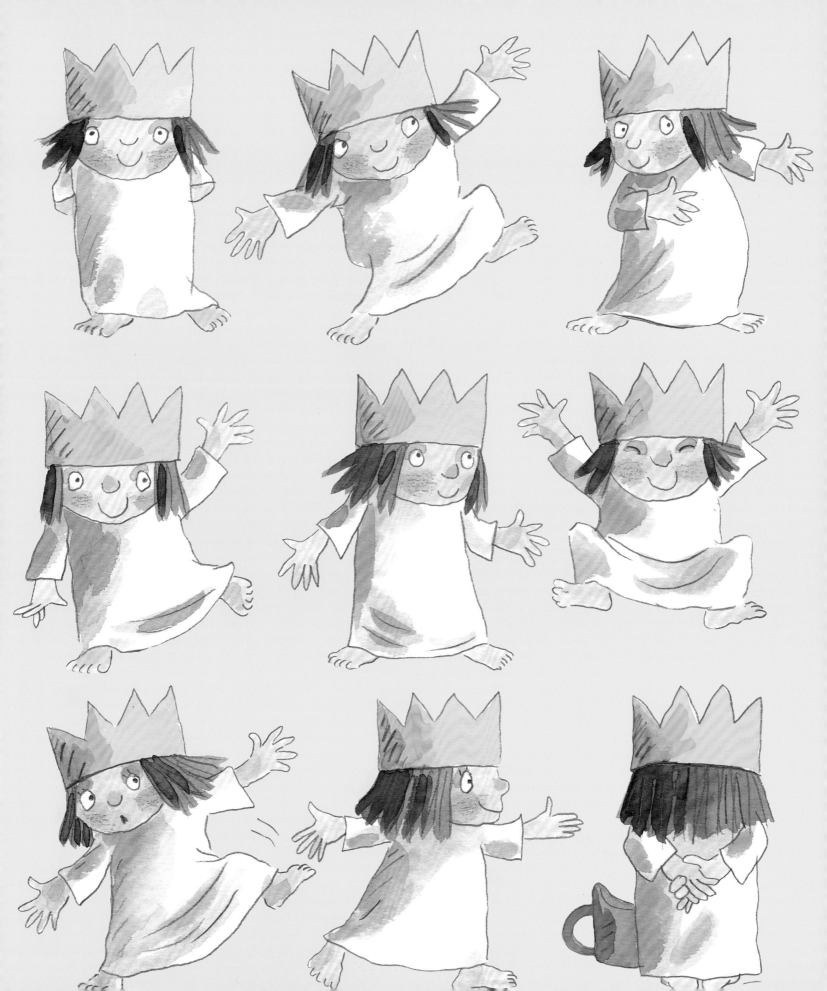

For Helen and her mad dogs

Copyright © Tony Ross, 2007

This paperback edition first published in 2008 by Andersen Press Ltd.

The rights of Tony Ross to be identified as the author and illustrator of this work
have been asserted by him in accordance with the Copyright, Designs and Patents Act, 1988.

First published in Great Britain in 2007 by Andersen Press Ltd, 20 Vauxhall Bridge Road, London SW1V 2SA.

Published in Australia by Random House Australia Pty., Level 3, 100 Pacific Highway, North Sydney, NSW 2060.

Colour separated in Switzerland by Photolitho AG, Zürich.

Printed and bound in China by Foshan Zhao Rong Printing Co., Ltd.

10   9   8   7   6   5   4

British Library Cataloguing in Publication Data available.

ISBN 978 1 84270 734 0 (Trade paperback edition)

ISBN 978 1 78344 016 0 (Riverside edition)

I Want My Light On!

Tony Ross

A Little Princess Story

Andersen Press

The Little Princess loved a story at bedtime.

But she didn't like the dark.
"I WANT MY LIGHT ON!" she said.
"Why?" asked her dad.

"Because there are ghosts in the dark," she said.
"Probably under the bed."

"Don't be silly, there are NO such things as ghosts,"
said Dad. "And there's nothing under the bed."

"Don't be silly, there are NO such things as ghosts,"
said the Admiral. "And if there were, the General
would deal with them."

"Don't be silly, there are NO such things as ghosts,"
said the Doctor. "And if there were, all you'd have to
do is blow your nose."

"I WANT MY LIGHT ON ANYWAY!"
said the Little Princess.

"Why?" said the Maid.
"Look, Gilbert isn't afraid of the dark."

"I'm not so much afraid of the DARK!" said the Little Princess. "I'm sort of more afraid of ghosts."

"Don't be silly, there are NO such things as ghosts,"
said the Maid. "And if there were, they'd be very small,
'cos I'VE never seen one!"

"Yes, Gilbert, ghosts are probably very small,"
said the Little Princess.

"So we must be careful not to step on them!"

"Nighty nighty, sleepy tighty," said the Maid . . .
and she switched off the light.

"I bet ghosts are afraid of the dark as well,"
thought the Little Princess.

"OOOO!" cried the Little Princess.
"That sounds very much like a ghost!"

"OOOO!" cried the little ghost.
"That sounds very much like a little girl!"

So the Little Princess hid under her bed.

So did the little ghost.

"BOOOOOO!" said the Little Princess.

"OOOOOO!" said the little ghost.

And he ran all the way back to where he lived
at the top of the castle.

"MUM, MUM, I'VE SEEN A LITTLE GIRL!"

"Don't be silly," said his mum. "There are
NO such things as little girls!"
"I WANT MY LIGHT ON ANYWAY!"
said the little ghost. "Just in case."

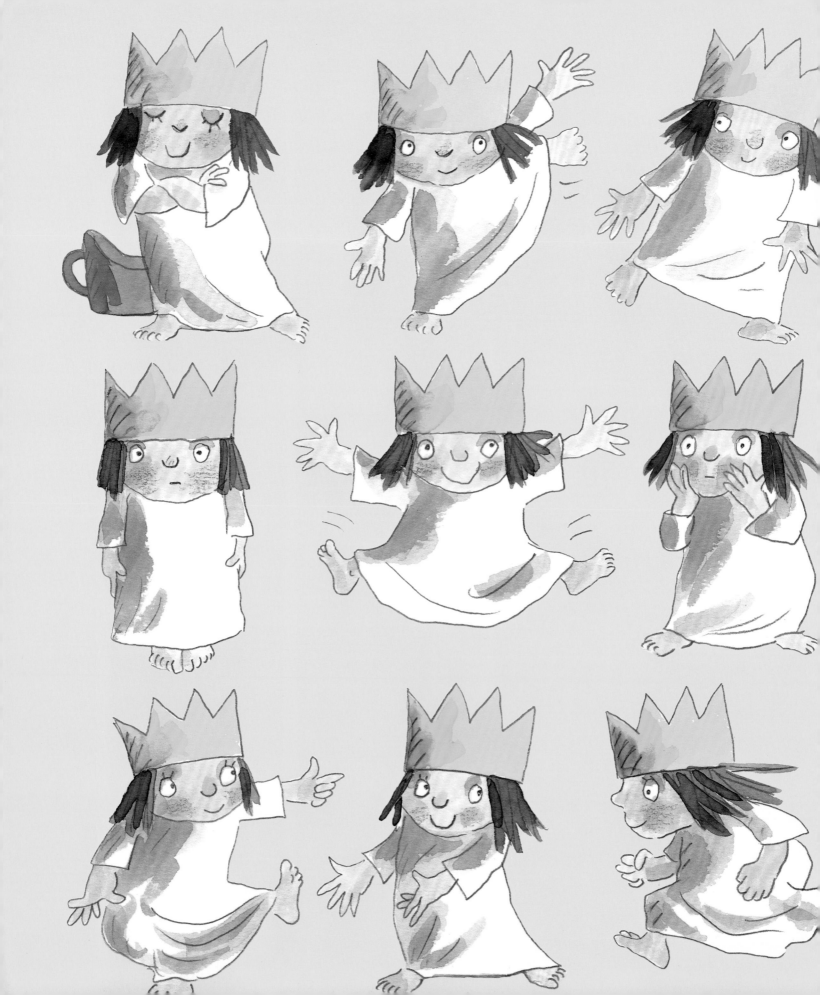

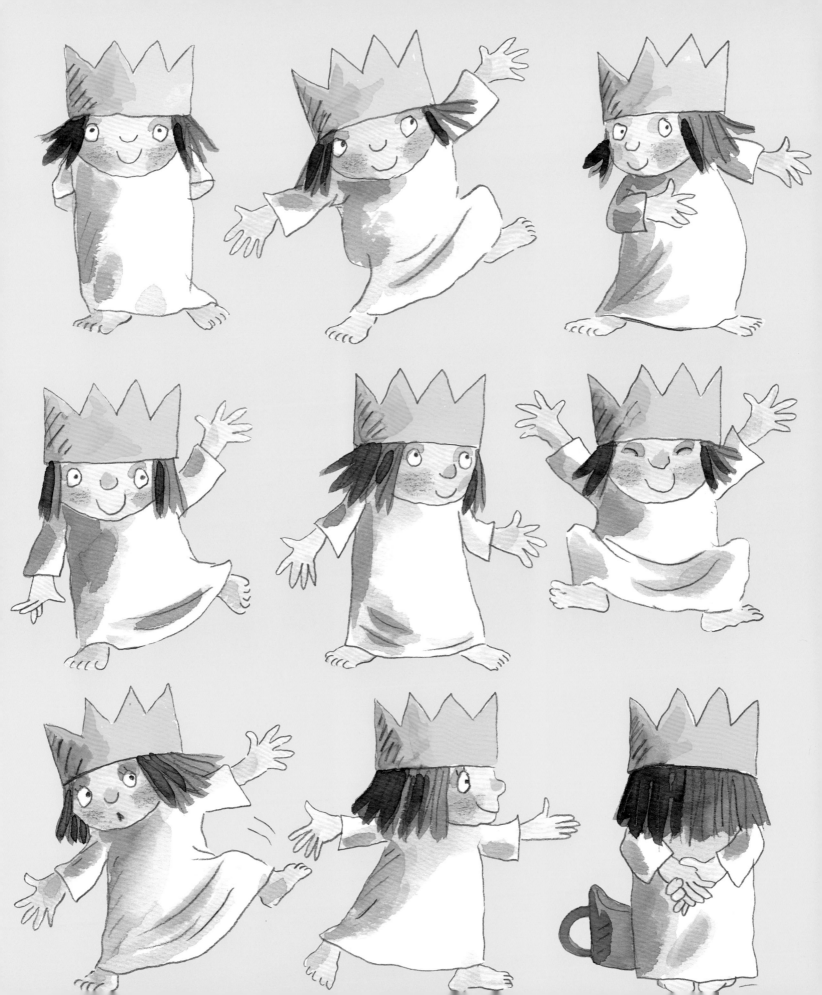

Other Little Princess Books

I Didn't Do it!

I Don't Want to Go to Hospital!

I Don't Want to Wash My Hands!

I Want a Boyfriend!

I Want a Party!

I Want a Sister!

I Want My Dummy!

I Want My Light On!

I Want My Potty!

I Want to Be!

I Want to Do it By Myself!

I Want to Go Home!

I Want to Win!

I Want Two Birthdays!

Little Princess titles are also available as eBooks.

LITTLE PRINCESS TV TIE-INS

Fun in the Sun!

I Want to Do Magic!

I Want My Sledge!

I Don't Like Salad!

I Don't Want to Comb My Hair!

I Want to Go to the Fair!

I Want to Be a Cavegirl!

I Want to Be Tall!

I Want My Sledge! Book and DVD